For Joseph, my son, my firstborn. — JB

For Mr. Won and Mrs. Lee, who gave me life, and for John and Pat, who gave me this world.
— AW

A Note from the Author

I've always loved the Nativity story, but when I first became a mother, I saw the holy family's miracle through new eyes, as I held my own firstborn son in my arms. Those memories, brought so tenderly to life by Annie's loving work, are this story's source, and my offering to the family of every miracle baby.

— Julie Berry

A Note from the Illustrator

Working with Julie on this beautiful story filled my heart with such great joy. My wish for every reader is that they, too, can be blessed with joy within the pages of this book.

— Annie Won

ISBN 978-1-338-27772-2 · 10 9 8 7 6 5 4 3 2 1 · 19 20 21 22 23

Printed in Malaysia 108 · First edition, September 2019 · The text type was set in Gabriela · Hand lettering by Angela Southern
Book design by Patti Ann Harris and Steve Ponzo

Long Ago, on a Silent Night

by Julie Berry

Illustrations by Annie Won

ORCHARD BOOKS

An imprint of Scholastic Inc.
New York

Long ago, and far away,
A baby was born on Christmas Day.
Shepherds knelt and angels sang
Till the night sky with rejoicing rang.
This wonder was seen by a lucky few.

I see a miracle in you.

Long ago, in a dusty barn,
A mother took a child in her arms,
Wrapped him snug, made his bed in the hay.
He was her gift that Christmas Day.
There's no sweeter gift than a life so new.

My best gift, little one, is you.

Long ago, at her child's first cry,
A mother sang a lullaby:
"Sleep, little angel. Sleep, little lamb.
When you need comfort, here I am.
I will always watch over you."

Hush, little babe, I'll sing it, too.

Long ago, with scarcely a sound,
The stable's animals gathered 'round,
Hoof and feather, hide and beak —
Some say the animals began to speak
Their love for the child. Could it be true?

We will whisper our love to you.

Long ago, on a silent night,
Travelers followed a new star's light
Bearing gifts of love to welcome a child
Who would one day calm a tempest wild,
And teach mercy and gentleness as he grew.

My love, you're a gentle teacher, too.

Long ago, at a temple door,
Simeon and Anna paced the floor,
Awaiting a glimpse of a promised son —
A prince of peace, a chosen one.

Before you came,
our family knew
it was worth the wait
to welcome you.

Long ago, so the carols sing,
Was born, to a maiden, an infant king,
With the sky for a palace, the earth for a throne.
The hills and the rivers, his treasures to own.

Through your eyes the skies shine a deeper blue.
Treasure of mine, you make all things new.

Long ago, as day followed day,
This baby grew in the usual way,
Watched and rocked and taught and fed,
Washed and dressed and tucked into bed.

We're blessed in the simplest things we do —
you return the love we give to you.

Long ago, at that sacred birth,
A piece of heaven fell to earth
To light the world and spread God's peace,
Bringing hope and help that would never cease.

From the moment I held you,
child, I knew, you came straight
from heaven, too.

Not long ago, in a nearby place,
Was given to me a gift of grace –
All my hopes, my joy, my heart's desire,
Your sweet voice is my angel choir.
Wondrous, holy, strange, and true –

Little one,
my miracle
is you.